The Ant and the Grasshopper

RETOLD AND ILLUSTRATED BY GRAHAM PERCY

The Child's World

For Alma

Distributed in the United States of America by
The Child's World®
1980 Lookout Drive • Mankato, MN 56003-1705
800-599-READ • www.childsworld.com

ACKNOWLEDGMENTS
The Child's World®: Mary Berendes, Publishing Director
The Design Lab: Kathleen Petelinsek, Art Direction and Design;
Anna Petelinsek, Page Production

COPYRIGHT

LIBRARY OF CONGRESS CATALOGING-IN-PUBLICATION DATA
Percy, Graham.
  The ant and the grasshopper / retold and illustrated by Graham Percy.
    p. cm. — (Aesop's fables)
  Summary: While an ant works hard all summer long to feed her children
and store food for the winter, her neighbor, a cheerful but lazy grasshopper,
relaxes in the sun.
  ISBN 978-1-60253-201-4 (lib. bound : alk. paper)
  [1. Fables. 2. Folklore.] I. Aesop. II. Grasshopper and the ant. English. III.
Title. IV. Series.
  PZ8.2.P435Ant 2009
  398.2—dc22
  [E]   2009001586

Prepare today for what you might need tomorrow.

here once was a busy ant—a very busy ant. Every morning, she got up before sunrise. She made breakfast for all of her children. Then she hurried out of the house with a huge sack over her shoulder.

All spring and summer, the ant hurried about. Every day, she collected grains and seeds until her sack was full. She worked until her feet and back were aching and sore.

The ant's neighbor was a cheerful grasshopper. But he was also very lazy. The grasshopper loved to relax in the sunshine. He liked to sing and chirp all day. He did not like to work.

One warm summer's day, the grasshopper stopped the ant. He thought she looked very tired.

"Why are you working so hard on such a lovely day?" asked the grasshopper. "Won't you join me for a picnic?"

The ant put down her heavy load and looked at the smiling grasshopper.

"I have no time for picnics," she said. "I need to make sure my family has enough food for the cold months ahead. You should be doing the same."

The grasshopper danced
around her.

"I don't have time for that,"
he laughed. "I want to enjoy the
summer sunshine."

The tired ant shook her head.
She slowly picked up her bundle
and went on her way.

Autumn came, and the ant was as busy as ever. She sorted all the food she had collected. She wove warm blankets for her children.

The grasshopper was still relaxing and enjoying the sunshine. But every now and then, clouds would appear. Sometimes the breeze would be chilly. Once in a while, the grasshopper would give a tiny shiver.

Soon it was winter. The wind was cold and the trees were bare. The ground was covered with snow.

But the ant's home was warm and snug. There was a cozy fire in the fireplace, and there were thick blankets on each bed. At every meal, her family's plates were piled high with food.

The grasshopper was very unhappy. He no longer sang or danced. He was cold. Worst of all, he was very, very hungry.

The grasshopper went to the ant's house. He shivered as he knocked on the door.

"May I please have something to eat?" he asked the ant.

The ant looked at the grasshopper in amazement. "I worked hard all summer long to gather food for my family," she said. "All you did was dance and sing. If you don't work in the summer, you can't expect any food in the winter."

The grasshopper hopped sadly away. The ant gathered her children close to her.

"Let the grasshopper's laziness be a lesson to you," she warned them. "Always prepare today for what you might need tomorrow."

AESOP

Aesop was a storyteller who lived more than 2,500 years ago. He lived so long ago, there isn't much information about him. Most people believe Aesop was a slave who lived in the area around the Mediterranean Sea—probably in or near the country of Greece.

Aesop's fables are known in almost every culture in the world, in almost every language. His fables are even *part* of some languages! Some common phrases come from Aesop's fables, such as "sour grapes" and "Don't count your chickens before they're hatched."

ABOUT FABLES

Fables are one of the oldest forms of stories. They are often short and funny, and have animals as the main characters. These animals act like people. Often, fables teach the reader a lesson. This is called a *moral*. A moral might teach right from wrong, or show how to act in good, kind ways. A moral might show what happens when someone makes a poor decision. Fables teach us how to live wisely.

ABOUT THE ILLUSTRATOR

Graham Percy was a famous illustrator of more than one hundred books. He was born and raised in New Zealand. He first studied art at the Elam School of Art in New Zealand and then moved to London, England, to study at the Royal College of Art.

Mr. Percy especially loved to draw animals, many types of which can be found in his books. He illustrated books on everything from mysteries to lullabies. He was even a designer for the animated film "Hugo the Hippo." Mr. Percy lived most of his life in London.